CAMILA
THE GAMING STAR

written by ALICIA SALAZAR
illustrated by THAIS DAMIÃO

PICTURE WINDOW BOOKS
a capstone imprint

Published by Picture Window Books, an imprint of Capstone
1710 Roe Crest Drive, North Mankato, Minnesota 56003
capstonepub.com

Library of Congress Cataloging-in-Publication Data
Names: Salazar, Alicia, 1973- author. | Damião, Thais, illustrator. | Salazar, Alicia, 1973- Camila the star.
Title: Camila the gaming star / by Alicia Salazar ; illustrated by Thais Damiao.
Description: North Mankato, Minnesota : Picture Window Books, an imprint of Capstone, [2022] | Series: Camila the star | Audience: Ages 5–7. | Audience: Grades K–1. | Summary: Camila wants to buy a camera, stand, and a microphone to record for her WeTube channel, and her brother suggests that an upcoming video game tournament might be the way to get the money she needs. But Camila does not play video games, and though her family supplies what she will need to practice, she only has a month to perfect her gaming skills—and that may not be enough to win. Includes discussion questions, glossary, and related activity.
Identifiers: LCCN 2021033237 (print) | LCCN 2021033238 (ebook) | ISBN 9781663958723 (hardcover) | ISBN 9781666331196 (paperback) | ISBN 9781666331202 (pdf)
Subjects: LCSH: Hispanic American girls—Juvenile fiction. | Video games—Juvenile fiction. | Contests—Juvenile fiction. | Brothers and sisters—Juvenile fiction. | CYAC: Video games—Fiction. | Contests—Fiction. | Brothers and sisters—Fiction. | Hispanic Americans—Fiction.
Classification: LCC PZ7.1.S2483 Caj 2022 (print) | LCC PZ7.1.S2483 (ebook) | DDC [E]—dc23
LC record available at https://lccn.loc.gov/2021033237
LC ebook record available at https://lccn.loc.gov/2021033238

Designer: Hilary Wacholz

Printed and bound in the USA. PO4608

TABLE OF CONTENTS

MEET CAMILA AND HER FAMILY................................4

SPANISH GLOSSARY................................5

Chapter 1
THE GOAL................................7

Chapter 2
THE CHALLENGE................................11

Chapter 3
WIN OR LOSE................................17

Meet Camila and Her Family

Spanish Glossary

difícil (dee-FEE-seel)—hard

domingo (doh-MEEN-goh)—allowance

gané (GAH-neh)—I won

juego (HOO-eh-goh)—game

me rindo (meh REEN-doh)—I give up

torneo (tohr-NEH-oh)—tournament, contest

Chapter 1

THE GOAL

"I need a camera, a stand, and a microphone," said Camila.

"For what?" asked Papá.

"For my WeTube channel," said Camila.

"You should save your **domingo**," said Papá.

Camila sighed.

It would take forever to save up enough money.

"There is a video game **torneo** next month," said her brother, Andres. "The prize is three hundred dollars."

Camila perked up.

"That is more than enough to buy what I need!" she said.

Then her shoulders sank.

"I don't know how to play video games," she said.

"I have an old laptop you can use to learn," said Papá.

"I have a controller you can use with the laptop," said Andres.

"I have a membership to StreamHouse," said Ana. "You can play some games for free."

Chapter 2

THE CHALLENGE

Camila started playing the next day after school.

A minute after she began, Camila lost.

"Game Over," said the computer.

She wrinkled her nose. "I can do better than that," she said.

She tried again.

"Game Over," it said again.

"Game Over."

"Game Over."

"It's on," said Camila.
She pushed up her sleeves
and hit *Start*.

"No **juego** will defeat me!"
she said. "I'll be the best gamer
in the world by next month."

She wandered into a magical forest and then . . . Game Over.

GAME OVER

"I'll be the best gamer in the whole city," she said, mostly sure of herself.

She wobbled on the edge of a blazing volcano and then . . . Game Over.

After three weeks, Camila put down the controller. She walked into the living room. Her family was watching a movie.

"**Me rindo**," said Camila. She sunk into the sofa. "I'll never be a real gamer."

"You still have a week until the **torneo**," said Papá. "Are you sure you want to quit?"

"I can't stand it anymore," said Camila. "I dream about trolls. I dream about battles."

"Maybe your brain is practicing," said Andres.

"But I keep losing in my dream," said Camila. "I just want to read a book."

"Maybe taking a break will help you decide," said Mamá.

Chapter 3

WIN OR LOSE

Camila picked up her favorite book, *The Secret Garden*. She read it all weekend.

She dreamed of seeds and robins and hundreds of flowers.

In between reading, she went to the **mercado** with her parents. She played with her cat, Pancho. She went to the park.

Monday morning, she felt
rested and refreshed. But she still
didn't know what to do about
the tournament.

Monday afternoon, Papá
got an email from the **torneo**
leaders.

"It says you need to be at the gaming room by 10:00 a.m. on Saturday," said Papá.

"Do you still want to quit?" said Mamá.

Camila bit her lip. How could she be a star if she kept losing?

She didn't care about the money anymore. She cared about doing the right thing.

She wanted to do what a star would do.

A star wouldn't quit just because something was **difícil**.

She stood up straight. "I'm going to do it," she said.

She started up her laptop.

She faced a
monster and . . .
Game Over.

She battled
a giant and . . .
Game Over.

A dragon
charged her
shield and . . .

Victory!

"**¡Gané! ¡Gané!**" she ran to tell her family.

"Whoop! Whoop!" they said and gave her high fives.

The big day arrived.

Camila sat in front of a gaming system. She worked hard.

Her avatar dodged and struck
and jumped and flipped.

But . . . "Game Over."

Camila didn't win the prize money. But she saved her allowance.

And in six months . . .

"Welcome to my WeTube Channel," she said to her video camera. "My first topic is 'How to be a video game star, even if you lose.'"

Design a Video Game Monster!

Camila faced scary beasts in her video game. Imagine you are a video game designer, and your job is to come up with a dangerous monster for a new video game.

WHAT YOU NEED
- white paper
- several colors of paint
- googly eyes
- glue
- markers
- feathers, buttons, glitter, or other decorations (optional)

WHAT YOU DO
1. Fold one sheet of paper in half, then open it and lay it flat. Squirt different colors of paint on one side of the crease.

2. Refold the paper and squish the sides together. Open it to see your monster shape. Let it dry.

3. When dry, add any details you want to your monster. How many eyes does your monster have? Do you need to draw arms, legs, or other body parts? Add other decorations if you want.

4. On a separate piece of paper, write some details about your monster's personality. Be sure to give your monster a name and list its strengths and weaknesses.

Glossary

allowance (uh-LOU-uhns)—an amount of money given regularly for a specific purpose

avatar (AV-uh-tar)—a character made to stand in for a person on a video game

controller (kuhn-TROH-ler)—a piece of equipment used to control the actions on a video game

microphone (MYE-kruh-fone)—an instrument used to capture sound waves so they can be recorded

victory (VIK-tur-ee)—a win in a game or contest

volcano (vol-KAY-noh)—a mountain with vents through which molten lava, ash, and gas may erupt

Think About the Story

1. Camila entered the video game tournament for the prize money. She did not want to save up her allowance for the equipment she wanted. Is it hard to save money for something big? Why or why not?

2. In what ways did Camila's family help her get ready for the video game tournament?

3. Do you think Camila was playing video games too much? Explain your answer.

4. Were you surprised about the ending of the story? Why or why not?

About the Author

Alicia Salazar is a Mexican American children's book author who has written for blogs, magazines, and educational publishers. She was also once an elementary school teacher and a marine biologist. She currently lives in the suburbs of Houston, Texas, but is a city girl at heart. When Alicia is not dreaming up new adventures to experience, she is turning her adventures into stories for kids.

About the Illustrator

Thais Damião is a Brazilian illustrator and graphic designer. Born and raised in a small city in Rio de Janeiro State, Brazil, she spent her childhood playing with her brother and cousins and drawing all the time. Her illustrations are dedicated to children and inspired by nature and friendship. Thais currently lives in California.